THE GINGERBREAD MAN

Written by Saviour Pirotta

Illustrated by Karl Newson

There was once a little old woman. She was hungry so she fetched some flour, butter and sugar, and made a gingerbread man.

This book belongs to:

....

....

Quarto is the authority on a wide range of topics.

Quarto educates, entertains and enriches the lives of our readers—enthusiasts and lovers of hands-on living.

www.quartoknows.com

Author: Saviour Pirotta
Illustrator: Karl Newson
Designer: Victoria Kimonidou
Editor: Ellie Brough

© 2017 Quarto Publishing plc
First published in paperback in 2019 by QED Publishing,
an imprint of The Quarto Group.
T (0)20 7700 6700 F (0)20 7700 8066
www.QuartoKnows.com

A catalogue record for this book is available from
the British Library.

ISBN 978 0 7112 4450 4

Manufactured in Shenzhen, China PP082019

9 8 7 6 5 4 3 2 1

She gave him raisins for eyes and cherries for buttons.

When the gingerbread man was baked, the old woman opened the oven. To her surprise, the gingerbread man jumped out and ran through the door.

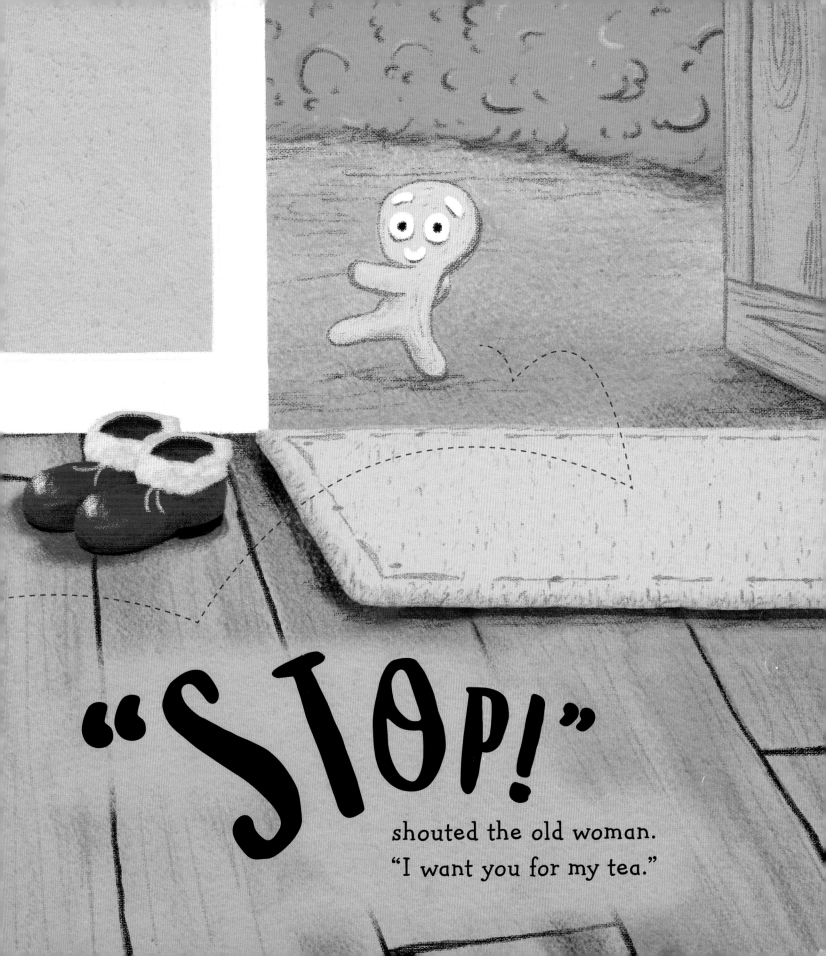

"STOP!" shouted the old woman. "I want you for my tea."

But the gingerbread man replied...

"Run, run, as fast as you can.
You'll never catch me.
I'm the gingerbread man."

A cow saw the gingerbread man running past and mooed,

"STOP!

I want you for my lunch."

But the gingerbread man shouted,

"Run, run, as fast as you can.
You'll never catch me.
I'm the gingerbread man."

So the
old woman...

and the cow...

chased after the gingerbread man
but they couldn't catch him.

A pig saw the gingerbread man going by and grunted,

"STOP!

I want you for my supper."

But the gingerbread man sang,

"Run, run, as fast as you can.
You'll never catch me.
I'm the gingerbread man."

So the
old woman...

the cow...

and the pig...

chased after the gingerbread man
but they still couldn't catch him.

Then the gingerbread man
came to a river.

"How will I ever get to the
other side?" he cried.

"Hop on to my tail,"
said a crafty fox.
"I'll carry you across."

The gingerbread man hopped on to the fox's tail.

The fox said, "You're getting wet there.
Why don't you sit on my back?"

So that's what the gingerbread man did.

Then the fox said,
"You're going to fall off
there. Why don't you
stand on my nose?"

So that's what the
gingerbread man did.

When they got to the other side, the fox flipped the gingerbread man up in the air with his nose and...

SNAP!

"STOP!"

cried the gingerbread man.
"That's half of me gone."

The fox flipped him
up a second time.

"STOP!"

cried the gingerbread man.
"That's almost all of me gone."

The fox flipped him up a third time and...

That was the end of the gingerbread man.

NEXT STEPS

Discussion and Comprehension

Ask the children the following questions and discuss their answers:
- What did the little old woman need to make the gingerbread man?
- Why do you think the gingerbread man was trying so hard to stay out of the river?
- Which of the characters do you like the best? Can you say why?
- What could the little old woman have done to stop the gingerbread man running away?

Learn about verbs

Ask to the children to say the repeating rhyme in the book:

Run, run, as fast as you can. You'll never catch me. I'm the gingerbread man.

Explain that 'run' is a verb. A verb describes an action or something that we do.

Give an example of changing the verb:

Hop, hop, as fast as you can. You'll never catch me. I'm the gingerbread man.

Get the children to do the action. Ask them to change the verb to make a new rhyme.

If able they could write out the new rhymes using full stops and capital letters.

Create a gingerbread man

Give the children a range of coloured paper and a template if needed.
Ask them to cut out all the shapes needed to make their own gingerbread
man – body, eyes, buttons etc. Once they have cut out the shapes
they can assemble with glue on a white sheet of paper.
These can be displayed with the rhymes from the activity.